Dedicated
to the
pupils and staff of
Innishannon National School

CONTENTS

The Author

Stephanie Dagg

Stephanie Dagg lives in Innishannon, County Cork.

She is married to Chris and is mother of two children, Benjamin and Caitlín, and has been writing stories ever since she was a child. Originally from Suffolk in England, she moved to Cork in 1992.

INTRODUCTION

Welcome to the Stone Age!

Flint Dog is set in the Stone Age about 25,000 years ago, when people had begun to use flint for tools and weapons. The proper name for the Stone Age is the Palaeolithic Period – but Stone Age is probably easier to say!

People moved out of their caves and began to live in villages of tent-like huts. They lived as hunter-gatherers. The men would hunt animals for meat and the women would gather nuts and berries. In *Flint Dog* the men are called Hunters and the women are called Birth-givers.

The hero of the story is Youngest, the youngest child in his family. There is no record of what people actually called themselves all those years ago. So, extending the practice of people taking their surname from their trade or occupation (which has given rise to many modern names such as Smith, Baker and Carpenter), the characters in *Flint Dog* have been named in a similar way. Youngest's father is called Flint Maker as he makes the flint tools for the tribe, and his mother is called Bread Maker because she is the best in the village at grinding corn between two heavy stones. There is Pot Maker, Lamp Maker and Strong Man, the village chief, to give a few more examples. Of course the children are too young to have a particular trade or skill, so they are given names that reflect some feature. Youngest, as we have just seen, is the youngest of his family. His older brother, who is the eldest child, is called First Son. Youngest's sister is called Hazel Eyes, because of her unusual light brown eyes. (Most of the villagers' eyes are dark brown.) Youngest's friends have names like Long Legs, Red Hair and Burnt Arm.

The story is based in France. The village setting was inspired by Les Eyzies in the Dordogne, a known stronghold of Cro Magnon people. (Cro Magnon is the name given to the people who lived at the time of this story. They were very much like us.) There is a river that runs in front of the village and large cliffs, riddled with caves, loom behind it. The holy cave mentioned in the story is based on the famous Pech-Merle cave in Cabrerets, Lot-en-Quercy. All the paintings described in *Flint Dog*, including the handprints on the walls and the footprints on the floor, can still be seen there today.

The Stone Age people worshipped the Mother Goddess, a sort of mother nature figure. They believed that she was responsible for the changing seasons and the various natural events that occurred, like floods or thunderstorms or deaths. She looked after the spirits of people and animals that died. She could be kind but she could also be very cruel.

That's all you probably need to know before you start to read *Flint Dog*. I hope you will enjoy the story and perhaps it will make you think about how our ancestors lived, all those many thousands of years ago.

Stephanie Dagg

WOLVES

'Wolves! Wolves!'

The shout rang out in the dark night. At once the sleeping village awoke. Dogs began barking and Hunters began shouting.

Youngest peered sleepily out of his corner in his family's tiny hut. By the light of the moon, he could see Father and First Son throwing off their goatskin blankets as they hastily rose and grabbed their axes. White Tail, their trusty dog, was ready for action too.

'Youngest, are you awake?' asked Father.

'Yes, of course!' cried Youngest, leaping up at once. Did Father want him to come and fight the wolves too? Youngest hoped so.

'Good. Then take your axe and guard the Birth-givers until we return.'

'But Father!' Youngest pleaded, 'can't I come too?'

'No, you are not yet old enough to be a Hunter. You must protect your mother and Hazel Eyes.' And with that they were gone.

'Aren't we worth protecting?' smiled Mother, sensing Youngest's bitter disappointment.

'Oh, of course, I didn't mean that,' said Youngest, ashamed. 'I just wanted to go with the Hunters.'

'I know, I know,' soothed Mother. 'But when you are a Hunter, you face many dangers. Tonight the Hunters are going to fight with hungry wolves that have smelt the dead bear and goats stored in the caves behind the village. It'll be a hard fight. Don't be in a hurry to face wild animals, Youngest.'

'No, Mother,' muttered Youngest. Still frustrated, he stationed himself by the door with his axe. Birth-givers just didn't understand. It would be brilliant to be a Hunter! Hunters weren't scared of anything.

Youngest listened to the shouts of the hunting group. He heard the dogs barking and the wolves howling. It sounded like a fierce fight. He tried to imagine taking part in it. He slashed an imaginary wolf with his flint axe and the sharp blade glittered in the moonlight. Father had made the axe. He made all the axes, spears and arrows for the village people. He had a special skill which made him very important.

Youngest glanced around at the collection of huts that was his village. They were made from branches, reeds and animal skins. Outside most of them sat the small and sometimes sleepy figures of Youngest's friends, keeping guard over the Birth-givers and small children. They were all as disappointed as Youngest at not being able to join in the fight.

Youngest gazed out into the moonlight. The village was situated on a high ledge of rock in front of cliffs that were riddled with caves. The Hunters used the caves to store the animals they killed. The meat was kept cool in the caves until the village people needed it. Usually the hoard was safe from wild animals. But not tonight.

Gradually the noise from the caves began to fade. Eventually the Hunters returned. Youngest saw that several of them were helping one of the Hunters to walk. So it had been a fierce fight! For a moment he felt anxious, but then he saw Father and First Son approaching.

'They're back, Mother!' he called. Mother rushed thankfully to the door to welcome the Hunters home.

'First Son did really well and helped kill two of the wolves!' said Father proudly. First Son glowed with pride.

'Two!' shouted Youngest, enviously. 'You're brave! I wish I was a Hunter like you!' And he really did. He wanted to make Father proud too.

First Son smiled happily. 'Huh, it was easy!' he boasted.

'Tell me, tell me!' begged Youngest, but suddenly he stopped jumping around in excitement. Where was White Tail? Usually, he came bounding in and licked Youngest when he got back from hunting.

'Father?' Youngest turned to the tall, strong Hunter. Father knew what Youngest was about to ask. He knew just what great friends his youngest son and the dog were. White Tail and Youngest played together every day and then curled up together every night under Youngest's goatskin blanket. Father knelt down beside his son and put an arm around him.

'Don't worry!' he smiled. 'White Tail is coming. It was a hard fight and White Tail is an old dog now. After a day's hunting, and a night's fighting, he's weary – like the rest of us! And he certainly fought hard. He saved me from a wolf tonight. A wolf was dragging away one of the goats so I tackled it. But another wolf jumped on top of me. The first one turned on me as well. I was hacking and kicking but I'm not sure I could have managed to deal with both of them. They were vicious. And that's when White Tail came to my rescue. He leapt in and killed one wolf straight away. He tore its throat right out. The other wolf turned on him but

I killed it. White Tail saved me. He's a good dog. Look – here he comes now!'

Youngest sighed with relief at the sight of his old friend. He darted out to welcome the limping dog with a hug. White Tail was panting hard. Youngest grabbed one of Mother's clay pots and rushed down to the river to scoop up some cooling water for the tired animal.

When he got back, he found Mother fussing around Father.

'Bring the water here,' ordered Mother sharply. 'Father is hurt. Quickly, I must clean the wound or it will go bad.'

Just for a moment, Youngest wanted to say that the water was for White Tail who was old and tired. Hazel Eyes, his sister, could go and fetch some more water for Father. But just then a shaft of moonlight fell on Father's wound and Youngest saw the dreadful gash. Poor Father! The young boy felt guilty at once and handed over the water straight away. He knew that Mother was right. Hunters quite often died of wounds that became infected.

'Hazel Eyes, run to Healer Man for some of his willow bark poultice. Here, take him this bowl of berries in exchange. First Son, are you hurt too?' Mother asked anxiously.

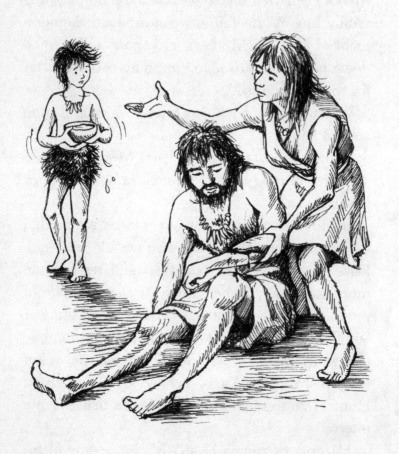

'No, I'm fine.' First Son sat down wearily. 'Poor old White Tail,' he said to Youngest. 'He's as old as I am, you know, and that's old for a dog.' Youngest was surprised at his brother's kindness. Now that he was a Hunter, First Son usually didn't have a lot of time for Youngest.

'Father said we'll get another puppy which can be yours,' First Son went on. 'Cow Keeper's bitch will have pups soon. Father's already asked him for one.'

Youngest felt another pang of guilt. His Father had thought to ask for another dog for him when he was tired and injured after fighting against wolves. And Youngest hadn't wanted to let him have the water he'd fetched. However much he loved White Tail, he loved Father much, much more.

Youngest crept over beside Father. He was horrified to see how badly Father had been bitten. His left forearm was torn and bleeding.

'Father, I'm sorry you got hurt,' he whispered.

Father's eyes twinkled. 'There's a brave Hunter! Mother has told me how you stayed by that door with your axe to guard them. I'd have pitied any wolf that tried to get past you! Now go and get that poor old dog of ours some water quickly. I'll be just fine.'

Youngest dashed off once again. Mother coated Father's wound with some of the strange smelling mixture Hazel Eyes had brought back from the Healer Man. Then Youngest returned and made a nest for White Tail next to his own sleeping place. He spread one skin out for White Tail, gave him a long drink of water and then the two friends settled down for the night.

A USEFUL ACCIDENT

Youngest woke as sunlight crept into the hut through the entrance. He rolled over and stretched out an arm to stroke White Tail, digging his fingers into the long silky fur. But he gasped and drew his hand back quickly. Instead of feeling warm, White Tail's fur was as cold as ice. Youngest hesitantly felt his friend again. White Tail's body was hard and stiff. The Mother Goddess had called White Tail's spirit away while he slept.

Youngest began to sob. Mother woke and saw at once what was wrong.

'Don't cry, Youngest,' she soothed. 'White Tail is with the Mother Goddess now. He'll never be tired again. Don't be sad.'

But Youngest found it hard not to be sad. He missed his special friend already. Father and First Son were rather quiet too when they saw White Tail's dead body. He had been a good and brave hunting dog and would be hard to replace. They took White Tail's body away to lay it to rest in the woods. Youngest didn't go with them.

When they came back Father set about making new weapons. Quite a few had been lost in the previous night's fight.

Youngest loved watching his father at work. First of all, Father would find a round stone, usually from the river bed. Then he would take a lump of the special rock called flint and strike it with the stone. With deft blows Father would start by removing any odd lumps and bumps. He knew exactly where to hit the flint. Then he would strike off a series of flakes from around the edge of the flint. This gave it a sharp edge. Then Father would take a smaller stone and would use it to chip away at the edge of the flint again, making it even sharper. It took Father a long time to make even a small arrow head. But Father's flint tools and weapons were said to be the finest for miles around. Visiting tribes

would trade furs or seashells or baskets and pots for Father's handiwork. Their own chief valued Father very highly. Father promised he would teach First Son and Youngest his skill when they were old enough.

That day, the village was full of the night's happenings. As soon as his jobs were done – collecting water for the day from the stream in the large earthenware pots that Pot Maker made and collecting wood for cooking – Youngest headed up to the caves with some of his friends. They gazed in awe at the bodies of the dead wolves that the Hunters hadn't yet skinned. Youngest's friends were impressed, but Youngest felt a lump in his throat when he saw the place where his canine friend had fought his last fight. However, he couldn't let his sorrow show in front of the others so he bit his tongue and said a silent prayer to the Mother Goddess to protect his faithful dog in the after-life.

'Come on, let's play wolf fights!' suggested someone.

'Yes, let's!' Youngest cheered up at once. He loved playing wolf fights. 'I'll be a wolf!' he shouted.

'Me too!' called out Burnt Arm.

Until they had grown old enough to acquire a skill or do something noteworthy that they could be named after, the youngsters had nicknames based on some distinctive feature. One friend was called Burnt Arm because he had crawled into a fire when he was a baby and had a badly scarred arm. Another friend was Long Legs because he was so tall, and another was No Words because he never spoke.

The boys roughly divided into wolves and Hunters and scampered into a cave. They fought energetically and eventually ran and tumbled back towards the village, close to the house of Basket Maker. Outside her house were several rows of baskets in various stages of completion. There were the plain baskets woven out of reeds – they were at the first stage of the process. Then there were the baskets she had just covered in wet clay, and finally there were the finished baskets, with dry hard clay on them.

Youngest had once asked his mother why they were covered in clay.

'The reed baskets are useful,' she'd explained, 'but when the baskets are finished with clay, it helps to stop the beetles and insects getting into the food inside them and spoiling it. It also means we can carry water in them too.'

The baskets were useful, but the clay wasn't very strong. The smallest knock or bump would make the clay crumble away. So Basket Maker was always busy.

The boys were too caught up in their game to notice the pots. A particularly energetic 'wolf' lunged at Youngest and the two of them rolled into the pots, knocking two, which were recently coated with wet clay, into Basket Maker's fire that burned nearby. It was a few minutes before the boys realised what they'd done, they were so busy fighting each other.

A strong smell coming from the fire made them stop and then they looked in horror at the pots sitting in the flames. The other 'wolf' turned and ran away. Youngest simply stood staring.

'Don't just stand there, take my baskets out!' came a shrill voice. Basket Maker had returned from gathering berries in the wood.

Youngest cautiously stretched his hand towards the flames. Yow! It was much too hot to touch. He looked around and saw a couple of large sticks nearby. Grabbing them, he prodded the pots and rolled them out of the flames. The pots were now a bright red colour.

'Look what you've done to my baskets!' scolded Basket Maker, squatting down beside the red-hot pots. 'Just wait till I tell your father.'

'I'm sorry,' apologised Youngest, hanging his head. 'Please don't tell Father. I'll help you gather reeds and make some more pots, shall I?'

Youngest actually quite enjoyed basket weaving – he'd done a little bit with his mother. Obviously he'd rather play with his friends but there were worse things to do than weave baskets.

'Shall I?' he asked again. He was a bit annoyed that his offer of help was being ignored. He looked up at Basket Maker. She was thoughtfully studying the baskets, tapping one of them with a stick, as it was still too hot to touch. The basket made a ringing sound, and – it didn't crumble. She tapped it again. The burnt basket seemed as hard as the rocks around them.

Youngest forgot to be humble and moved closer, his curiosity aroused.

'By the tall trees!' he exclaimed. 'The basket's really hard, isn't it?'

'Why yes, Youngest, it is!' smiled Basket Maker. 'I should be mad at you for knocking my baskets into the fire, but it seems to have improved them. It looks like they'll last a lot longer now that they've been cooked. I shall have to experiment with some more baskets. I wonder how long I should cook them in the flames. Now, let's see . . .' And with that she turned away from Youngest and began muttering to herself and selecting clay-coated baskets that were still wet. Youngest could see she'd forgotten all about him so he slipped away.

Smiling proudly and feeling rather pleased with himself, he set off to find his friends. Judging by the splashing sounds he could hear, they had gone for a swim in the river that ran below the rock ledge the villagers lived on.

The river was wide and slow flowing, and always so cool. Sometimes the river became angry and burst its banks. Only last year, a little child had been swept away by the fast running water and drowned. It had taken a lot of prayers to the Mother Goddess to restore the river to its usual calm self. Youngest shuddered a little as he thought of the might of the Mother Goddess. But then he caught sight of his friends and all thoughts of fear fled from his head. He had a lot of news to tell them!

YOUNGEST'S NEW PET

The villagers were soon all benefiting from the new, baked baskets. Basket Maker was very generous in saying how Youngest had helped her to make the discovery. By trial and error she had eventually hit on the best method and length of time for baking them. She showed all the Birth-givers how strong these new baskets were. Even the Hunters were impressed with this new invention.

A few days later Cow Keeper's bitch had her puppies, but the bitch was a poor mother and all but one of them died. And that puppy had to go to the village chief, Strong Man. So no new dog for Youngest. Youngest tried to put on a brave face, but he was very disappointed. He still missed White Tail very much.

Father felt sorry for Youngest. Then one day he had an idea. A new, sharp knife would take the boy's mind off dogs. So, he might be spoiling the child a bit, but what harm. Youngest was a good son and one day he'd be a fine Hunter. So Father set off for one of the good outcrops of flint where he

obtained the lumps he needed to make weapons. He poked around and filled his large goatskin pouch with some suitable stones. He was just turning to leave when his eye was caught by a very unusual looking rock. He stooped to look at it more closely. He smiled, then he laughed as he picked up the lump of flint. It was a knobbly, misshapen piece, no good for weapons – but it had the shape and form of a dog! It looked like a small, grey puppy! Here was a find indeed!

Squatting down on his haunches, he pulled his shaping pebble out of his pouch. It only took a few skilfully aimed blows to refine this stone animal. Father added eyes and tidied up the 'tail' a bit. Holding it up he admired his handiwork. Youngest would be thrilled.

Father hurried back to the hut. The evening meal was ready and the rest of the family were waiting for his arrival. Hazel Eyes scurried to fetch the basket of fruit and nuts she had gathered that day.

'Wait!' Father held up his hand importantly. 'I have a special present for Youngest.'

'What is it?' gasped Youngest in excitement. This was a real surprise.

'Well,' Father went on, 'since you can't have a puppy just yet, I thought I would make you a knife. But then I had another idea – and here it is!' With a flourish he drew his work of art out of his pouch. 'For you, my youngest son. This pup should last forever!' And with that he placed the stone dog in his son's outstretched hands.

For a few moments Youngest was too amazed to speak. All he could do was stare at this creation. It was incredible! It was brilliant!

'It's a flint dog!' he croaked at last.

Hazel Eyes and First Son crowded round to look. Even Mother came to inspect it too. They all murmured their amazement. Hazel Eyes couldn't help feeling jealous. Father saw her expression.

'Come here, pretty one!' he smiled. 'Next time the traders from the seashore come I'll be sure to get some shells from them to make you a necklace.'

Hazel Eyes' face shone with pleasure. 'Oh thank you, Father! Mother, did you hear that? I'm going to have a shell necklace, just like you.'

'Well, you'd better give your father a big hug then, to say thank you!' laughed Mother.

Father disappeared under a flurry of arms and flying hair as Hazel Eyes ran to hug him. Youngest laughed at the sight, and even First Son allowed himself to smile.

'Thank you for my dog, Father!' Youngest beamed his appreciation as soon as Hazel Eyes had finished her cuddle with Father. 'I shall call it Flint. Can I go and show it to my friends now?'

'No,' said Father firmly. 'Now it is time to eat and then we have to do the evening jobs. There will be time enough tomorrow!'

Tomorrow was a long time coming for Youngest. Curled up in his corner that night, he kept looking at Flint. And when it got too dark to look any more, he gently stroked the rounded contours of the stone animal. He was too happy to sleep!

Next day, Youngest was the envy of all the other

children. He showed them Flint and spent most of
the day swaggering around with a gaggle of
children at his heels. Later that afternoon Father
found that his favourite spot for finding good
lumps of flint had been invaded by children, all
searching for strangely shaped rocks. Soon all the
children of the village were carrying animal-
shaped rocks around. Long Legs had what he said
was a fish, and Red Hair had a deer. The other
children had horses, cows and even birds. Some of
them didn't look much like animals at all, but no
one minded. Flint was by far the best, though!

AN ANGRY GODDESS

Next day the Hunters went on a hunting trip. The bear and goats had all been eaten now, so it was time to replenish supplies. The Hunters were very excited as Spear Maker had invented a new weapon. It consisted of a light hunting spear with one of Father's sharp flint heads on it, and a sort of throwing device. This was a short piece of bone. The Hunter held it at one end and placed the handle of the spear in the other. The throwing device effectively made the Hunter's arm longer so he could throw his spear further. This meant there was less danger of being hurt by the animals they were chasing. If it worked successfully, it would help the Hunters greatly.

Father and First Son left with the other Hunters at dawn. From his corner, where he lay snuggled up with Flint, Youngest sleepily watched them go. He drifted back into a deep slumber, dreaming of playing with a real live Flint. All too soon it was time to get up. Mother gently shook him awake.

'Remember, today we must plant the seeds for the bread-making plant,' she told him.

Youngest stretched and yawned trying to wake up. Boring! he thought to himself. He didn't enjoy planting and digging and things like that, although he knew how important they were for the village. They never managed to grow a great deal of the bread–making plant, but it saved a lot of time and effort spent seeking and then gathering the grains from wild plants. However, Youngest didn't say anything to Mother. She probably found it tedious too but she never complained. Everyone had to help in feeding the village.

After a meal of some bread and berries, the women and children gathered together on the plain in front of the settlement. The Hunters had

already cleared an area of ground ready for planting. The Birth-givers were carrying weighted sticks. These were sharp sticks with stones tied to the top with thin strips of leather. The extra weight made it easier to press the sticks into the ground to make a hole for the seed. The women walked in rows, punching the stick into the ground. Then the children would drop a seed into each hole and cover it with earth. It was tiring, hot work. Once the seeds were planted, they were left to grow on their own. The villagers would return when the ears of corn were ripe and ready for picking. Quite often the corn wouldn't have grown very well and the crop would be poor.

However, Father had said recently that one of the Hunters who was interested in plants thought that if they watered and maybe even spread some animal dung over them, the plants might grow better. He said he had noticed that wild plants grew better in rich, damp soil than in dry soil. Some of the Hunters had laughed at him.

'Mother Goddess makes the plants grow, not us!' they had said.

But Father had told Mother that he thought the Hunter was probably right – he'd noticed the same thing himself. Probably the corn plants needed nourishing, just like people did. Mother had agreed and said she would ask the other Birth-givers to help her water the plants every so often.

Youngest was soon very bored with his job. He obediently trailed along behind Mother dropping seeds in the holes, only he kept getting distracted. He wasted quite a lot of seeds. Mother got cross.

'Oh, get along with you, useless boy!' she scolded angrily. 'Hazel Eyes, you take over. We'll have an empty field if Youngest carries on like this.'

Hazel Eyes smiled in a superior way at Youngest who retaliated by sticking his tongue out at her. Then he grabbed Flint whom he'd placed safely out of the way at the edge of the planting area and ran off before Mother changed her mind.

Outside the field he found several of his friends hanging around. There were also some older boys that Youngest didn't know that well. At about ten or eleven summers of age, they were nearly old enough to be Hunters. The youngsters had either been sent out to play by their mothers or had sneaked off when no one was looking.

'Hi!' said one of the older boys as Youngest appeared. 'Just in time! We've decided to go to the holy caves for a look around.'

Youngest felt a surge of panic clutch his stomach. The holy caves! Only Hunters were allowed in there. Youngest knew that the Hunters did magic in those caves and painted magical pictures that brought good luck to the village. Those caves were very special places indeed. And besides, cave bears lived there! But Youngest didn't want these older kids to think he was scared. So he shrugged nonchalantly and said 'Fine!' But he gripped a bit tighter on Flint.

The boys set off for the holy caves, which were in another set of cliffs several thousand paces away from the village. A couple of boys ran back to the village to collect some lamps and fire stones. Youngest knew there would be trouble when the grown-ups found out that lamps were missing. But for now he was starting to enjoy himself.

It was a hot sunny afternoon. The boys played around as they walked through the thick oak woods, picking some berries and nuts if they found them. Suddenly, ahead of them through the trees appeared a sheer ridge of rock. This was the cliff of the holy caves. Youngest gasped at the sight. The mighty wall of rock soared up into the sky. This must truly be a magical place, he thought.

The path took them steeply downwards. The trees grew smaller and stunted and there were lots of boulders lying around. One of the older boys said that Mother Goddess threw these boulders down from the cliffs sometimes. Youngest hoped she wouldn't throw any while he was there! They crept further through the undergrowth towards the limestone cliff and finally the openings to the caves appeared before them. Youngest hadn't really known what to expect but he certainly hadn't expected such small, gloomy entrances. The boys gathered round one and peered in. They could feel the cool air of the cave already and it was damp at the entrance. The boys were all very quiet.

'Right then!' said someone. 'Time to light the lamps!'

Lamp Maker's son stepped forward. He had the fire stones. These were two pieces of quartz, one fairly large and the other smaller.

'Get me some dry grass,' he ordered importantly. Long Legs darted off to fetch some. Youngest moved in as close as he dared. He loved to see the flames come alive.

Lamp Maker's son squatted down. Long Legs came hurrying back with a handful of dry grass. Youngest wondered where he'd found that in this damp place. Lamp Maker's son nodded his thanks. He put some dry grass on the ground and then put the larger stone on top of it. Steadying it with one hand, he took the smaller stone in his other hand, then crack! he whacked the small stone down onto the other. A tiny chip of quartz flew off, but no sparks. Lamp Maker's son tried again, and again.

'I thought you could make fire,' grumbled one of the older boys.

'I can!' retorted Lamp Maker's son crossly. 'Just wait and see!'

He whacked the stone down angrily and this time a tiny spark flew off. It landed in the nest of dry grass. Lamp Maker's son immediately cupped his hands around the small, struggling flame. It flickered for an instant and almost died, but then it began to burn more strongly.

'Quickly, light the lamps!' called Lamp Maker's son. Two lamps were held out. One was made from a big piece of thick bone that had been shaped something like a big spoon. The spoon part of it was packed with hard animal fat. It had a wick in the centre that was made from twisted vegetable fibres. The other lamp was the same shape, but had been made from soft stone. The two wicks sputtered alight.

All the boys smiled.

'Off we go then!' said Lamp Maker's son. He led the way to the first cave. Youngest and Long Legs followed him closely. Youngest couldn't help shivering as he left the warm daylight world behind and crawled into the dark passage of the cave. He hoped they wouldn't upset the Mother Goddess by being so bold. He held Flint tightly to his chest.

Youngest's eyes soon got used to the gloom. The cave was bare and dull. The lamps cast their flickering light on the walls and roof, but there was nothing much to see.

'I don't see what's so special about these caves, do you?' he whispered to Long Legs. 'They're just the same as the food shelter caves by the village!'

Lamp Maker's son heard them. 'Just you wait!' he grinned. 'Just a bit further – and here we are!'

As he spoke, the boys turned a sharp corner and stepped into the most enormous cavern Youngest had ever seen. On all sides strange rock formations loomed over them – long needles of rock hanging from the cave roof and huge, pointed teeth of rock protruding from the floor. Youngest could see tall, thin pillars of rock that stretched from the floor right up to the roof.

'Roaring thunder!' he breathed, but it was a totally inadequate thing to say. There were simply no words to express the beauty and weirdness of this place.

Everyone looked around in wonder. Only Lamp Maker's son and one of the older boys had been there before, so it was all new to the other children.

'And that's not all!' grinned Lamp Maker's son again. 'Come and see the paintings.'

'But we're not meant to see those until we are Hunters!' protested Red Hair.

'Sissy! No one will ever know we've been,' said Lamp Maker's son. 'Well, you can stay here if you like, but the rest of us are going. Come on.'

He set off towards a corner of the cavern. They all followed except Red Hair. He stood hesitantly for a moment. He knew they were doing something they shouldn't. He knew he should go back outside. But it quickly became dark as the boys with the lamps moved away. Red Hair was terrified. 'Wait for me!' he called and hurried after the others as fast as he could. He slipped and banged his head as he went but he didn't stop till he was back in the pool of light from the lamps.

Lamp Maker's son stopped before a small hole in the wall.

'We have to crawl along here,' he said. Youngest's heart sank. He didn't like the idea of that very much.

'Hey!' said Long Legs beside him. 'This is really fun.'

Yes, it is, isn't it,' agreed Youngest half-heartedly. He didn't want his friends to think he was scared like Red Hair. So reluctantly he dropped to all fours, still clasping Flint, and then squirmed through the tiny passage on his belly. Ugh! It was cold and damp and painful. Flint kept digging into him too. It seemed an age, but it could only have been a few minutes, before the passage widened and they could stand again. Youngest rubbed his sore elbows and knees while they waited for the other boys to come through.

'Now, let's see the paintings,' said Lamp Maker's son. They followed him around another bend in the passageway, and then they all exclaimed together as Lamp Maker's son held up his lamp and revealed a smooth part of the cave wall covered in pictures of animals. These, Youngest knew, had been painted by Picture Maker. It was he who engraved figures of animals on some of the weapons and tools and who did these magical paintings which Youngest had heard so much about but had never seen until now. The paintings really were amazing. There were bison and horses, mammoths and bears. There were also a few shapes that Youngest didn't recognise.

'What's that?' he asked pointing to a sort of rounded, loopy blob.

'That's the Mother Goddess, you silly billy!' laughed Lamp Maker's son. 'Look, that's her belly and that's her bottom and . . .'

'Oh, I see now,' said Youngest, embarrassed.

They all looked in admiration. The animals were so lifelike. You could see the hair on the mammoths and the steamy breath of one of the bison. The paintings were colourful – black, red and brown.

'Look, what's this?' came Red Hair's voice. He was bending over some objects on the cave floor. Lamp Maker's son went over to investigate. He picked up a block of black rock, peered at it and then tentatively rubbed it against the cave wall. It left a smear of black.

'By the winds, it's Picture Maker's drawing rock,' he cried. He looked back at the other things Red Hair had found. There was a pile of reddish powder on a flat stone.

'I bet this is paint,' he said, scooping a little powder into one hand and then spitting on it. It mixed into a thick paste.

'Look, I can paint now!' he boasted. Dipping a finger in the mixture, he drew a wavy line on the cave wall.

At once all the other boys clamoured to make paint too. Youngest pounced on the drawing rock that Lamp Maker's son had discarded in favour of the paint. He tried to draw White Tail but his effort didn't look much like a dog at all. Then he had an idea. He held Flint up against the wall and drew round him with the black rock (it was a substance called manganese oxide, in fact). The result was much better this time. Youngest felt very proud.

He glanced around at the others. Long Legs and Red Hair were making hand prints on the walls. They were smearing their hands with paint and pressing them against the wall, giggling as they did so. Lamp Maker's son had climbed up onto a boulder and was painting red blobs onto the roof of the cave. The others were scribbling away busily.

What would the Hunters say next time they came here and saw all these new drawings? Youngest wondered anxiously. But no-one else seemed to be concerned so he carried on drawing too.

'I've found some mud over here,' came a voice. Youngest looked up and saw Burnt Arm standing in a far corner of the cavern. 'It's all squishy. I'm making footprints!'

Youngest and Red Hair went over to see. Sure enough, on the damp rocky floor there was a hollow of mud. Burnt Arm was prancing around in it, making loads of footprints. Youngest and Red Hair joined in the fun, digging their toes into the cold mud.

Suddenly there came a low rumbling noise.

'What's that?' squealed Red Hair in fright.

'It's the Mother Goddess!' cried someone. 'She's angry! Quick, let's go!'

The boys fled at once, pushing and shoving to get back through the tiny passage. In the crush, one of the lamps fell to the floor and broke. Now they had only one lamp between them and that one was growing fainter every minute. Youngest felt very scared indeed. He clung onto Flint to be sure that he didn't drop him in the panic.

Somehow or other they all managed to scramble out of the cave just as the other lamp burnt out. They all stood panting for a few moments, catching their breath after the mad dash. And then they heard another rumble, only this time it became deafeningly loud. The ground shook below their feet and a cloud of dust burst out of the cave entrance. Youngest and Long Legs clung to each other, too scared to run away like the others were doing.

'Whistling winds!' whispered Youngest in a very shaky voice, when the rumbling died away. 'Whatever was that?'

Long Legs cautiously walked towards the cave entrance. He peered into the gloom.

'Hey, Youngest, come and see!' he called.

Youngest crept forwards to join his friend.

'Look into the cave now,' said Long Legs.

Youngest did.

'I can't see the cave any more,' he said puzzled. 'Just a pile of rocks and stuff.'

'Yes, the cave has gone,' agreed Long Legs. 'The Mother Goddess has made rocks fall to block it up. I suppose we went a bit far with our messing around.'

'I think you're right,' said Youngest, pale and shaking. 'Thank goodness we got out when we did or . . . or . . .' His voice trailed away. It was too terrible to think what would have happened if they hadn't got out of the cave in time. But at least this way no-one would ever find out what they'd been doing in the cave.

47

'I'll make sure I never upset the Goddess again,' said Long Legs grimly.

'Me too!' nodded Youngest.

The two boys turned and walked silently home. They saw the other boys back in the village but they didn't dare speak about what had happened. Not one of them ever spoke about the afternoon's events again.

STRANGERS

The Hunters returned that evening with a bison and three deer — and something far more exciting. They had with them three Birth-givers from another tribe. The women looked quite different from the Birth-givers in Youngest's tribe. They were taller and slimmer, and had fairer hair.

Everyone gathered round to stare at them. The village chief, Strong Man, bustled importantly out of his hut to take charge of the situation.

'Stop staring!' he commanded. 'Let's show some welcome to these Birth-givers and hear their story.'

At once Mother and some of the other Birth-givers disappeared and came back with plates of berries and pots of water to drink.

The three newcomers knelt down and ate and drank gratefully. Strong Man squatted beside them and began to ask them questions. At first the Birth-givers just looked confused as Strong Man spoke. He tried different words to ask where they had come from. Suddenly one of the newcomers, the eldest one, smiled and began to speak. She

understood what he was saying at last. She spoke a slightly different language but she managed to explain that she was a mother and the other two women were her daughters. With tears in her eyes she told how her own tribe had been wiped out by the Battle-Axe warriors. When they heard this, all the Hunters began muttering and talking to each other. They had heard about these fearsome warriors before who came from a faraway land and killed everyone in their path. That was stupidity itself since there were so few people around anyway. There were enough enemies already with all the wild beasts to battle against – people didn't need to fight each other too.

The old Birth-giver continued to speak. She explained that the attack had happened a while ago, when the cuckoo's song could still be heard. Since then she and her daughters had travelled through the forests, living off berries and nuts and finding shelter where they could.

Today when they had heard the Hunter's voices they had hidden in terror thinking they were the Battle-Axe warriors come to kill them. Only when they had seen the Hunters, and realised that they were different people, had they shown themselves. They were so hungry and weary they knew they would not last much longer alone. She hoped the chief would allow them to join his tribe. In return they would work hard and her daughters would make fine wives for any Hunters who needed a mate.

Strong Man beckoned Father and Healer Man over to him. These were the two Hunters whom he valued and respected the most. The three men drew away to one side. They talked quietly amongst themselves, occasionally nodding towards the new Birth-givers.

While they were conferring, some of the village Birth-givers crept forward to look more closely at the strangers, and in particular at their unusual clothes. They wore skins like themselves, but their skins were joined together somehow, rather than just draped around and tied on with pieces of leather. These clothes looked warm and well fitting. Mother fingered the old woman's clothing, marvelling at it. The old woman felt her touch, and turned and smiled.

'Tomorrow,' she said in her strange accent, 'if we are allowed to stay, I will teach you and your friends how to sew skins, shall I?'

'Yes, please,' Mother smiled back. The woman nodded to her.

Just then Strong Man, Father and Healer Man came back to the others. Strong Man stepped forward and, smiling, held out his hands to the three Birth-givers.

'We welcome you to our tribe. Now we will feast together to celebrate the goodness of the Mother Goddess who has brought you to us. Our village needs more Birth-givers and we will take care of you as your own tribe would have done,' he announced.

The old woman burst into tears with relief. Someone clapped their hands, and soon all the villagers were clapping. Youngest didn't quite understand what was happening but he knew that everyone was happy that these Birth-givers had come.

That night the whole tribe gathered around a large fire and feasted on roasted meat and listened to stories that the Chief told. Some of the Hunters fetched their instruments and the evening ended with singing and dancing. Some played pipes made from animal bones with holes cut in them at intervals. Others hit mammoth tusks with pieces of wood. A few of the Birth-givers rattled strings of bones. These made a hollow, echoing sound. Youngest loved to hear the music. He sighed happily.

Eventually, it was time to sleep. The old woman and her daughters went to Basket Maker's shelter.

Basket Maker's husband had been killed the year before by a mountain lion while out hunting and she had been alone since then. She was glad to have company again. Father told Mother that the two daughters had already been claimed by two Hunters who needed wives. The Chief would hold the joining ceremony at the next new moon. Youngest was glad at the news. The joining ceremonies were great fun.

A STITCH IN TIME

Next morning Mother was full of excitement at the prospect of learning how to sew. She hurried everyone along over breakfast and the morning jobs.

'What's the rush?' grumbled Father as she practically pushed him out of the hut.

'I'm going to learn how to sew, that's what the rush is,' she retorted. 'Now, go to your axes.'

Father shrugged and set off for his favourite flint spot. Mother and Hazel Eyes made for Basket Maker's hut. Youngest tagged along at a distance. Several other Birth-givers joined the procession to meet with the old woman, all curious as to what was going on.

The old woman was waiting for them outside the hut. She already had two skins lying on the ground in front of her.

'Good morning,' said Mother politely.

'May the Goddess smile on you,' replied the old woman graciously. 'Now, first we need to make a needle to do the sewing.'

'And what is that made from?' asked Mother.

'Bone. I need a small piece of bone and a stone to shape it with,' said the old woman.

'Hazel Eyes, go and get me a bone and a stone from Father, quick now!' ordered Mother.

Hazel Eyes sped off at once.

'While she is gone, we can make the thread,' went on the old woman. She took a flint knife and carefully sliced a thin strip of leather off the edge of one of the skins. She turned it over and shaved the hairs off it with stroking movements of the flint blade.

'Now you try,' she said to Mother. Mother nervously took the knife and began to cut another thin strip. Her cutting was a bit crooked and she and some of the Birth-givers giggled.

'You'll get better,' said the old woman.

A loud panting and the thudding of feet announced Hazel Eyes' return. She was red in the face from running so fast. She carefully laid a handful of bones and a large, rough stone in front of the old woman.

'Thank you, my child,' smiled the old woman. Hazel Eyes blushed with pleasure.

The old woman selected the smallest bone from the pile and set to work filing it with the rough stone. The Birth-givers watched in silence.

Youngest was fascinated to see the shavings of bone flutter down to the ground. The piece of bone became thinner and thinner. The old woman only shortened it a little. It was now about as long as Youngest's hand and as fine as a stalk of corn.

The old woman then filed carefully at one end.

'What are you doing now?' Youngest couldn't help asking.

'I'm sharpening it, curious one!' she smiled. 'How does this feel?'

And with that she pricked him very gently on his hand.

'Ouch!' yelped Youngest in surprise. The Birth-givers laughed. Youngest frowned, but when the old woman winked at him, he stopped feeling quite so cross.

'Last of all, I need to add an eye to the needle,' explained the old woman. She took the flint knife again and sliced into the other end of the needle. Youngest could see now that this end was a little broader and flatter than the rest of the needle. After a few deft strokes, a hole appeared.

'There!' exclaimed the old woman. 'Now we can sew.'

The Birth-givers watched breathlessly as the old woman took her needle and one of the strips of leather. She tied a knot in one end and threaded

the other through the needle's eye. Next she
skewered one of the skins near the edge with the
needle and pulled it right through. The leather strip
followed it. Then the old woman did the same to
the second skin. This time as she pulled the leather
strip through, it pulled the two pieces of skin
together. The Birth-givers gasped in amazement.

The old woman laughed. 'That's all it is! You just carry on sewing along the edges of the skins you want to join. Remember to tie a knot when you have finished sewing to hold the thread tight.'

She handed the needle to Mother. Mother carefully inspected the old woman's stitch. Then she had a go. She drove the needle into the first skin.

'Ow!' she cried, and dropped the sewing. There was a bright red drop of blood on one of her fingers.

'You must be careful with the needle,' warned the old woman.

Mother tried again. This time she was more careful where she held the skin. She did a perfect stitch. And another. Then she handed the sewing to another Birth-giver. They all had a go, even Hazel Eyes.

'Thank you,' said Mother when they had all tried. 'This is a wonderful thing you have taught us. We are very grateful.'

The old woman nodded and turned to go back into the hut. Mother and the others hurried away to prepare the noontime meal. The morning had flown by.

GOOD LUCK

The village chief was very pleased to have the new Birth-givers in his clan. They had brought new blood and new skills to his tribe, both of which were very valuable. He knew that he must thank the Mother Goddess for this good luck.

But more luck was to come. A few days later, some of the villagers were woken by a lot of noise coming from the river which flowed close to the village. A few Hunters grabbed their spears and went to investigate. There in the shallow water close to the bank was a mammoth with its tusks tangled in a fallen tree! It must have got caught up when it came to drink. Father sent First Son back to the village to get more Hunters and tell them to bring their new throwing spears.

Most of the tribe hurried down to the river to see the spectacle. It was the first time Youngest had seen a real, live mammoth. He gazed in amazement at the huge creature. It was enormous and looked so fierce with its long hairy coat and huge sharp tusks.

He stood with Long Legs and Red Hair and watched as the Hunters attacked it. Standing on the bank, they rained their spears down on the creature. The mammoth roared with pain and struggled to free itself, but it was stuck fast. Youngest almost felt sorry for the trapped animal, it was so striking. But that one mammoth would feed the villagers for weeks, and the skin would clothe them all. The tusks and bones would be useful too, for weapons and tools.

The animal soon lay dead, and then began the difficult task of dragging it out of the water. It took the Hunters most of the day to get the mammoth back to the bank. Then they began to skin it and carve up the flesh to carry it bit by bit to the village. Youngest and all the children spent the afternoon carrying meat in baskets up to the storage caves. The Birth-givers built a huge fire in the centre of the village to roast some of the meat that night. It would be a double celebration because tonight there was a new moon and the new Birth-givers, whose names were Dawn and Moon – rather strange names, Mother said – would be joined with their husbands. Youngest loved joinings because there was lots of music and dancing. The first bit of the ceremony was very dull – Spirit Man said lots of funny sounding words.

Apparently they were special words that the Mother Goddess understood. But once all that was over, then the fun began.

Sunset seemed a long time coming. Everyone had worked very hard all day, but they were about to get their reward. The mammoth meat had been roasting on the fire much of the afternoon and the village was filled with the most delicious smell. The Birth-givers had been collecting nuts and berries, and even some beautiful flowers to scatter around the fire. The important Hunters, like the village chief, Father, Healer Man and Spirit Man put on their special clothes. These consisted of cloaks of pale, rich mountain lion skin, and special head-dresses of skin with deer's antlers. Youngest hardly recognised his father, he looked so different. All the Hunters painted themselves with red and yellow paints, but the two Hunters who were about to be joined to the Birth-givers were more or less covered with paint. As for Dawn and Moon, they were painted too, but more gracefully. They had been given jewellery made from bones and seashells by the two Hunters, and the Birth-givers had woven flowers into garlands for them. They looked beautiful, Youngest thought.

Just as the sun was about to dip out of sight, everyone gathered expectantly around the fire.

Spirit Man stood up and called the two couples to him. He then began the speaking part of the ceremony. Youngest found the speech boring and whispered to his friends while this was going on. Then Spirit Man joined the hands of each Hunter with his new female mate and the fun started. Everyone cheered and the musicians began to play. The mammoth meat was dragged out of the flames and big chunks were carved off for everyone.

Youngest ate so much he could hardly move! He certainly couldn't dance so he just had to watch as the members of his tribe jumped and twisted around the fire. The flames threw weird shadows against the huts and the cliffs. It was a little bit scary. Youngest wriggled close to Mother.

'Isn't this fun!' he said.

'Yes, this has been a good day,' agreed Mother. 'The Mother Goddess has been very good to us. We must thank her.'

'How will we do that?' asked Youngest. He felt he ought to say a special thank you to the Goddess for forgiving him and his friends so quickly for what they'd done in the holy caves.

'Well, the Hunters are talking about setting a huge stone in the earth in her honour. What do you think of that?' she replied.

Youngest wasn't sure what he thought. It didn't sound very exciting. If he were the Goddess he'd much rather have a nice axe or a piece of mammoth meat than a big stone. Presumably the Goddess liked big stones.

'That sounds nice,' he said dubiously.

Mother smiled. 'Ask your father to tell you about it tomorrow. Now, if you'll let me get up, I'm going to dance.'

And with that she joined the other figures

weaving around the flames. Youngest watched his mother for a while, but it was hard to make her out in the flickering light and he soon lost her in the melee of twirling, whirling bodies. His eyes gradually grew heavier and heavier. He dozed off and dreamt about a mammoth dancing on top of a huge stone right outside his hut.

A ROCKY SPOT

Next day the whole village was alive with talk of the big stone, or menhir as they called it. The chief, Father and a few other Hunters had seen some menhirs when they had journeyed to another tribe some time ago to trade some weapons for skins. This faraway tribe had erected huge single standing stones and also some smaller ones in long rows. Youngest heard that there was a lot of discussion going on in his village about what would be best. In the end, the chief decided they should erect one large stone, the largest they could find. Father was chosen to search for a suitable menhir.

He spent many days searching but each night he returned home tired and unsuccessful. One day Father took Youngest with him and Youngest, of course, took Flint. Mother gave them some cooked meat, bread and nuts to take with them. Youngest carried the food in the new skin pouch that Mother had made for him. She was always sewing things these days using the new bone needle the old woman made for her. Father teased her about it, saying that he didn't dare sit in one place too long or Mother would probably sew him to it! But Youngest knew that Father was really very proud of Mother's new ability which was making quite a difference to them. Their sewn clothes were much warmer, and the sewn pouches much stronger than anything they had had before.

Youngest was thrilled to be out with Father. They headed out through the woods, past the holy caves (so far no-one had yet discovered that the caves had become blocked up – Youngest hoped it would stay that way) and on into territory that was new to Youngest. It was rocky ground with a few stunted trees and bushes. They trekked a long, long way but Youngest was too happy to feel tired. As they walked, Father chatted to him about the plants and birds they saw. They paused for a drink at a gushing stream. Father pointed out a few shining fish to Youngest.

'Let's catch some for Mother!' exclaimed Youngest.

'No!' laughed Father. 'They are too small to bother with. Leave them and they'll grow big and fat, and then they'll be worth catching.'

'Can we come back when they're big, then?' asked Youngest. He would love to go fishing with Father.

'Of course we can,' smiled Father. 'When the leaves have fallen from the trees, that will be the time to come back. Don't forget now!'

As if Youngest would forget a treat like that! Youngest beamed happily and they set off again.

They began to climb upwards. Soon the landscape changed again and became more barren. Now there were just a few thorny bushes around and there were large rocks everywhere.

'Surely one of these will suit our purpose,' panted Father, stopping for a rest. 'Let's eat now and then we'll search around here.'

'Good idea,' agreed Youngest who was starving. He took the meat and bread Father handed him and looked around for a likely spot to sit. He noticed a rocky ledge behind a thorn bush. Carefully edging round the bush he jumped up onto the ledge.

'I'm going to sit up here, Father,' he announced proudly.

'Fine,' said Father, squatting down on the rocky ground. 'Just don't fall off or your Mother will sew me up and throw me in the river!'

Youngest giggled and walked a few paces along the ledge. It wobbled.

'Oh!' he gasped. 'The ledge is moving!'

He took a pace back and the ledge wobbled again.

Father was up in a second, arms outstretched to pull Youngest down. As he lifted him to safety, he looked at the ledge.

'Actually Youngest,' he said, 'I don't think it is a ledge. Let me see.'

He pulled his big axe out of his pouch and slashed away at the thorn bush. He used the handle of the axe to ease the cut branches away from the rock.

'Well, well,' he muttered examining the rock some more.

'What? What is it?' cried Youngest.

'This isn't a ledge at all, it's a huge boulder,' announced Father excitedly. 'And what's more, it's the perfect shape for our menhir. See how long and even it is. Youngest, you've found our menhir!'

'Yippee!' shouted Youngest and began dancing around. Didn't he have something to tell his friends now? Unfortunately he trod on one of the thorny branches Father had cut down and that stopped his dancing. He sat down and pulled the thorns out of the thick skin on his feet.

Father was still studying the rock. 'Hmm, it will take a lot of work to get it back to the village, but it will be worth it. This menhir will please the Mother Goddess, that's for sure.'

He turned to Youngest. 'Let's finish our food and

then we'll go back to the village and tell everyone our good news.'

Youngest bolted his meal down, and as soon as Father had finished too, they started to make their way back. However, after just a little way Father stopped and picked up a few large stones.

'Youngest, find some more stones like these,' he ordered.

'Why do you want stones, Father?' asked Youngest as he scrabbled around, searching for rocks.

'We must mark our trail so that we can find our way back to the menhir,' explained Father. 'I'm sure we'd remember it anyway, but to be on the safe side we'll leave some piles of stones to guide us. When we get to the woods, I'll make marks on the trees with my axe.'

'By the clouds, you are clever, Father,' said Youngest admiringly. 'When I'm a Hunter, will I be as clever as you?'

'Much, much cleverer, I expect,' smiled Father, taking the stones Youngest had found. 'We'll leave a pile of rocks like this every thirty paces.'

THE CHIEF

It took a long time getting back, making a trail as they went. It was almost sunset when they arrived back in the village. Father went straight to Strong Man's hut.

'Shall I go home?' asked Youngest, thinking Father had forgotten about him.

'No, you can come with me. After all, you found the menhir,' replied Father.

Youngest suddenly felt very nervous. Strong Man was such an important man and Youngest had never really been anywhere near the village chief before. Now he was about to go into his hut and speak to him!

'Can't you tell him you found it, Father?' suggested Youngest.

Father chuckled. 'Strong Man is a wise and brave man, and he's also very kind. You need never fear your chief. He cares for us all and every single one of us is important to him, especially you little ones.'

'Why especially us, Father?' asked Youngest.

'Because one day you'll be the Hunters, and one

of you will be the new chief. You are our future. You'll go on and discover new things to make your lives easier and our tribe bigger. That's very important indeed.'

They arrived at the chief's hut, which was bigger than the other huts in the village. There were huge mammoth's tusks around the doorway. Youngest thought they looked magnificent. One day I'll build a whole hut out of mammoth's tusks and bones, he thought to himself.

Father called out to Strong Man. The chief's wife rushed out and ushered Father and Youngest in. Like their own hut, it was very gloomy inside, but as Youngest's eyes adjusted to the lack of light, he noticed that it was full of fine fur skins. Whereas he had a goatskin for sleeping, the chief had wolfskins and bearskins. There were many spears and axes propped up against the wall. Youngest gazed around in amazement. Strong Man smiled when he saw the young boy's wonder.

'So, how would you like to be a chief like me?' he asked Youngest.

Youngest nearly jumped out of his skin. He'd been completely engrossed, wondering at the finery of the hut. For a second he was too surprised to speak. He hugged Flint tight to make himself brave. Then he saw Father looking at him expectantly so he quickly pulled himself together.

'It would be brilliant,' he bubbled enthusiastically. 'I'd have a hut just like this one except it would be made from mammoth bones. Oh, and my wife would be younger than yours,' he added without thinking.

Then, as he caught Father's horrified expression, he realised what he'd said. How could he have been so rude? But Strong Man and his wife burst out laughing. His wife came forward and hugged Youngest.

'I hope she will be younger than me!' she chuckled. 'My sons are Hunters now and my daughters have sons and daughters of their own. It would be a shame if you had to join with an old Birth-giver like me!'

'I didn't mean to be rude!' muttered Youngest, looking down and turning bright red in the face with embarrassment. He fiddled with Flint.

'You are not rude, you are honest, and I respect honesty,' answered the chief, still smiling. 'And what is this?' He gently took Flint from Youngest's hands.

'This is my flint dog,' said Youngest proudly. 'White Tail died and there weren't any new puppies so Father gave me a dog made of stone. He's called Flint.'

Strong Man inspected Flint carefully.

'He is a very handsome dog indeed.' He smiled
as he handed Flint back to Youngest.

Then he turned to Father.

'So, what news of our menhir?'

'The best news! Youngest here jumped onto a
rocky ledge to eat his noontime meal and

discovered that it was not a ledge at all but a boulder. And I am convinced that it is the ideal boulder for our menhir. I have marked a trail and I will take you to see it tomorrow at sunrise. I truly believe our search is over.'

'Well,' Strong Man turned to Youngest, 'it seems you are not only honest, but clever too. You have found our menhir. I think I will have to watch you carefully or I'll wake up one day and find the village has a new chief! Well done, Youngest.'

He laid his hand on Youngest's head. It was Youngest's proudest moment.

'And well done, Flintworker. I know how hard you have toiled in searching for our sacred stone. Tomorrow we will go and see what you have found for the Mother Goddess.'

And with that, Father and Youngest left the chief's hut.

'Father, I— ' began Youngest once they were outside, wanting to apologise for his big mouth.

'It's all right, son,' Father interrupted him. 'The chief is very pleased with you. Now, let's tell the others of our discovery.'

THE MENHIR

Mother, First Son and Hazel Eyes were thrilled at the news about the menhir. They darted off to tell their friends and soon the whole village knew that Youngest had found the menhir and had then told the chief that he'd like a hut made of mammoth bones and a young wife. Youngest's friends were green with envy. Swaggering around importantly with Flint in his hand, Youngest basked in all the attention.

Next day, Father, Strong Man, Lamp Maker and some other Hunters set off early to see the menhir. The whole village waited excitedly for their return. Everyone found it hard to concentrate on their chores that day. Youngest was supposed to be helping Mother scrape some skins but he just couldn't keep his mind on the job. He kept thinking about his menhir. What if the chief didn't like it? Would he be cross with Youngest and Father?

He was so preoccupied that he wasn't any help at all to Mother and she sent him off to play and called Hazel Eyes to help instead. Hazel Eyes had been practising sewing with some of her friends and wasn't too pleased at having to go and scrape smelly old skins.

But Youngest needn't have worried. When at last the Hunters returned, the chief was smiling broadly. He summoned the tribe at once and announced that the menhir had indeed been found.

'Tomorrow,' he said, 'we will begin preparations to bring the menhir to the village. It will take a lot of hard work, but the Mother Goddess has been good to the village and so it is only right that we honour her in this way with our efforts.'

Then the Hunters who had been to view the menhir disappeared into the chief's hut to discuss how to bring the menhir to the village. The others drifted back to their huts, talking about the huge task that lay ahead.

The family waited impatiently for Father to return home that evening. As soon as he walked in, Youngest and Hazel Eyes bombarded him with questions.

'How will we get the menhir here, Father?'

'Will it take long?'

'Can I help?'

'Will we have a feast when it's here?'

'How heavy is it?'

Father laughed. 'Stop, stop!' he cried, putting his hands over his ears. 'Let's eat our meal and then I'll tell you what the plans are.'

The meal went on for an awfully long time. Youngest had never realised what an age Mother and Father took to eat a meal. The couple kept chatting and laughing. And then Mother insisted on Father having second helpings. We'll be here all night! thought Youngest grumpily. But at last the meal was finished.

Father yawned and stretched.

'Now, what did you want to know about the menhir?' he asked.

'Everything!' Hazel Eyes spoke for all of them.

'Goodness, where do I start?' sighed Father. 'Right. The facts are that Youngest's menhir is many, many paces from here. It is also very heavy. There is a big, thick wood between here and the menhir and some rough, rocky ground. It will be hard to bring it back to the village.'

'So how will we do it?' asked First Son.

'We will need many ropes. Tomorrow, Strong Man has said, we will begin making ropes. We will use plaited leather strips and plaited vines. The Birth-givers will cut the skins and the Hunters will gather vines from the woods. Everyone will help to plait them. Other Hunters will go hunting every day for our food of course, and also for extra skins. Then, when the ropes are made, we will fell trees from the wood.'

'Of course! To make a path for the menhir!' burst out Hazel Eyes.

'Exactly,' nodded Father. 'But also to provide rollers for the menhir.'

'What are rollers, Father?' asked Youngest puzzled. He couldn't think how trees would help move a menhir.

'We will lay the rollers under the menhir. That will make it much easier to move the boulder than just dragging it along over the ground. Some of us saw this being done when we visited the distant tribe with the many standing stones. What happens is this—'

Father pulled a stone out of his pouch, and picked up a few twigs from the floor. He laid the twigs in a row and then put the stone on top of them.

'With our ropes, we will pull the menhir along, like this.' He moved the stone forwards. 'See, it moves along. The stone is actually rolling along on the rollers.'

'It's left a twig behind!' pointed out Hazel Eyes.

'That's right. Now, I take this twig – our roller – and put it in front of the stone. So as the stone carries on moving, it slides onto this roller.'

'And another roller gets left behind,' observed Youngest.

Father nodded again. 'And that's how it works. As the stone slides forward and leaves a roller behind, that roller is moved to the front of the stone to allow it to carry on moving. And so on and so on until we get the menhir here.'

But Youngest had a question.

'How will we get the menhir onto the rollers to start with?' he asked.

'A good question, Youngest. It won't be easy. We will have to use strong tree trunks to raise the menhir up so that we can slide the rollers underneath. That's probably the trickiest and most dangerous part.'

'And how will we set the menhir in the ground so that it stands up, like the stones you told me about?' asked First Son.

'Again, it will be difficult,' said Father. 'We will have to dig a pit for the menhir to stand in first and roll the stone right up to it. Then we will use tree trunks again to lever the stone up so that one end slides into position in the pit. We will use ropes too. We need to build a frame from tree trunks and place it on the side of the pit away from the menhir. Using ropes that loop through the framework we can help to pull the menhir up as well as lever it in from behind.'

Youngest wasn't quite sure that he understood the last bit but he did understand what an enormous job lay ahead for them all.

'I'll help as much as I can, Father,' he promised.

'And so will I,' said Hazel Eyes.

'I know you will,' smiled Father. 'Now, off to sleep so that you are strong and fresh tomorrow for making ropes.'

FLINT DOG

The next day Youngest helped to make ropes until his hands hurt. And the following day, and the day after that. Youngest even dreamt about making ropes in his sleep. But soon there were enough ropes for the job.

First Son helped to fell young, healthy saplings. The Hunters chose the straightest ones they could find to make the best rollers. Mother and the other Birth-givers cut skins into thick strips. Even Hazel Eyes helped. Everyone in the village worked very hard.

And then the job of bringing the menhir to the village began. The Hunters set up a temporary camp near the menhir while they worked on raising it and setting it on rollers and on clearing a trail through the wood. Father was gone for the whole time between new moon and full moon. A few Hunters stayed with the Birth-givers and children to guard them and hunt for food for them. One or two Hunters returned from the camp most days to bring news of what was

happening and collect fresh bread from the Birth-givers.

Youngest wished he could be with the Hunters. He felt he ought to be. After all, he found the menhir. He really should be there to help. The more he thought about it, the more annoyed he got. For a couple of nights he even thought about sneaking off in the moonlight to see what was going on. But he knew that the darkness brought danger of wild beasts. And anyway, with Father and First Son gone at the moment, Youngest was the Hunter of the house. The Birth-givers needed him.

But at last the menhir was coaxed onto the rollers, and ropes tied around it and the task of dragging it to the village began. It took a long, long time. The hot weather ended, the leaves fell from the trees and the time of the frosts began, and still

the Hunters wearily pulled the menhir, day after day, steadily closer to the village. Now that they were nearer, the children and Birth-givers could go and watch. Youngest marvelled at the power of the Hunters. He saw how their muscles bulged and their veins stood out as they heaved and heaved. He watched as the huge stone glided forward, bit by bit, on the tree rollers. He even helped a few times to carry the rollers from behind the menhir to be put in front of it again.

Meanwhile, work was beginning in the village on the site for the menhir. The chief had chosen a site at one end of the village, half way between the holy caves and the river. Some Hunters dug a huge hole using flint axes and big flat stones to scoop the earth out. Meanwhile Father supervised the building of an enormous framework of tree trunks next to the hole. This would be used to help pull the menhir up into position, just as he had explained to Youngest and the rest of the family that night, so long ago now.

At times Youngest almost grew tired of the menhir. Everyone worked so hard, life wasn't much fun any more. Father was always weary in the evenings. He was often cross because he was so exhausted. Mother was busy too as new ropes were constantly needed. Youngest had to help scrape the skins, and he hated that. The fat on the skins smelt so horrible. And when he scraped it off with a sharp flint tool, bits of fat got under his fingernails and made his hands feel all greasy.

He had to wash in the river every night, and now that it was getting colder, he came back freezing. It took longer every day to thaw out in front of the fire. He hardly had any time now to play with Flint and there was certainly no time to play with his friends. They were all just as busy as he was.

But finally, at long, long, last the menhir arrived in the village. The chief announced a feast that night to celebrate. It wasn't a very big feast as only a few Hunters had been out hunting every day while the others pulled the menhir, and so they hadn't managed to bring much meat home. And there were no berries or nuts any more. But in spite of this there was enough food to go round and plenty of bread. Most people were too tired to dance and make music, but at least they felt happy that the task was nearly over. The following day would see it completed.

At sunrise next day, the village was a hive of activity. The menhir was dragged the last few paces to the edge of the hole. Father and some other Hunters looped new, strong ropes around the menhir and then tied them onto the wooden framework, leaving long ends trailing down which they could pull. Some more Hunters brought strong tree trunks for levering the menhir up and moving it into position.

At noon the chief gave the order to raise the menhir. Spirit Man appeared in his strange costume with antlers on his hood and intoned prayers to the Mother Goddess. The villagers gathered to watch. Father and some other Hunters heaved on the ropes that hung from the frame. Others pushed down on the tree-trunk levers. At first nothing happened. Then, amidst the creaking of the wood and the grunts and gasps of the Hunters, the menhir began to tilt upwards. Youngest gasped too and clutched Flint tightly.

Degree by painful degree, the menhir tilted more. Then at last it was teetering on the edge of the pit. Finally, with a mighty thud, it slid down into the hole. A cheer went up from the villagers.

But the celebration came too soon. The pit was not quite deep enough to hold the menhir securely. The huge boulder wobbled first towards Father and the wooden frame, and then back towards the Hunters who had been levering it into position, eventually toppling towards the side of the pit.

'Quick!' roared Father. 'We need more Hunters to help here!'

Everything now depended on using the ropes to pull the menhir into place securely. Hunters and even Birth-givers raced to help. They grabbed the ropes and pulled with all their might. The wooden frame creaked under the strain as the menhir slowly, slowly became more upright.

'Just a bit more, then it will be balanced!' yelled the chief, himself heaving on the ropes with the others. 'Start filling in the hole on the far side of the menhir to help hold it up!'

This job fell to the remaining Birth-givers and children. Most of the soil that had been dug out when the pit was made lay in piles on the ground around it. Now, using their hands and their feet, the women and children shovelled it back around the menhir. It seemed to be working. Youngest shovelled for all he was worth, but the next moment something clouted him heavily on the side of his head and he fell sideways.

'Ow! Who did that?' he yelled, looking up. And then he froze. He saw what had hit him – one of the ropes holding the menhir up had snapped and whiplashed back.

'By thunder, the menhir is falling!' someone screamed.

Youngest glanced up. Sure enough, the huge boulder was slowly toppling again. Youngest felt a rush of fury. His menhir was not going to fall. He wouldn't let it! It wasn't going to happen.

He scrambled to his feet. The Hunters were desperately hanging on to the remaining ropes, trying to keep the mighty stone erect. Youngest looked into the pit. Surely if they could just get enough stones and soil to this side of the menhir, that would be enough to keep it up.

'Keep shovelling!' he heard himself screech. Everyone had stopped to gaze in horror at the toppling stone. 'Come on, quick!'

He pedalled his own legs furiously to kick soil into the pit. Others did the same. But still the stone was toppling.

'Just a bit more!' called a voice.

But all the soil was gone! Some had been moved

away from the pit by the Hunters earlier. They thought they had left enough to fill it once the menhir was in place.

They only needed another dozen rocks or so to hold the menhir up. Youngest looked wildly around. His gaze fell on Flint and the other rock animals that the children had left in a heap when they had hurried over to help. These toys were the only things near at hand. There was no time to fetch rocks from further away.

'Our animals!' he cried. 'Our rock animals! They'll do it!'

At that moment the menhir lurched menacingly as a few people let go of the ropes, unable to hold on another second.

Youngest dived towards the animals and scooped them up. A few of his friends did the same. Then, with a last look at his dear Flint, Youngest dropped him into the pit with the rest. The stone creatures were just bulky enough to hold the menhir steady.

'It's stopped moving!' cried the chief. Sure enough the mighty megalith stood firm and still. This time nobody cheered. No-one had the breath or the energy. They just sighed with relief that disaster had been averted.

The chief began to bark out orders to the Hunters nearby to fetch more rocks and earth.

Youngest watched in a daze as gradually the hole was filled in. He felt very dizzy from the blow the rope had dealt him and a bit light-headed from all his exertions. He sank to the ground.

'Goodbye Flint!' he whispered. 'Thank you for saving the menhir!'

'No – thank you,' said a voice in his ear.

Youngest looked up and saw the chief standing over him. Father was beside him, looking weary but triumphant.

'Your quick thinking and action kept the menhir up. You stopped it falling. You really are quite a Hunter, aren't you!' said the chief.

'Oh no,' blushed Youngest. 'I'm not a Hunter yet. I'm too young.'

'As and from now, you are a Hunter,' replied the chief, squatting down beside Youngest. 'You may be a bit young, but you have proved you are wise enough and brave enough to be a Hunter. And to celebrate your new title, I have a special present for you.'

'I—' Youngest was speechless.

He turned and called out something to his wife. She scuttled off and returned a few moments later holding a small bundle wrapped in a skin. She handed it to the chief.

By now the whole village had gathered to see what was going on. The chief began to unwrap the skin from the bundle. Suddenly a small, shiny, wet black nose appeared. Then a face followed. It was a puppy!

'My bitch had puppies a moon ago,' said the chief. 'I was going to keep them all, but then I remembered about your beloved White Tail. Now that you have given your little flint dog to save our menhir, you must have this dog. Here, he's yours.'

The chief pushed the little creature into Youngest's hands. Youngest couldn't believe it – his very own puppy! He wanted to jump for joy, only he was too dizzy and tired.

'Thank you!' he croaked at last. 'Thank you, thank you! And do you know what, I shall call him Flint too!'

The chief laughed and put his hand on Youngest's head again.

'So now!' he announced to the gathered tribe. 'We have our menhir and we have a new Hunter. Everyone will rest now, but at sunset we will honour the Mother Goddess here at our menhir and then we will eat and dance and make music all night long!'

The villagers cheered, and began to chatter happily about the day's events and what the evening would bring. Many of them had a few words to say to Youngest, congratulating him on becoming a Hunter and thanking him for saving the day.

Youngest was in a haze of happiness. He was proud of himself for saving the menhir and proud of himself for becoming a Hunter. But most of all he was proud of his new dog Flint – and his old flint dog.